Chinese Tale Series

中国神话

Hou Yi Shoots the Suns

后羿射日

Written by *Feng Jiannan*
Illustrated by *Chen Huiguan*

据中国古代神话

冯健男　改编

陈惠冠　绘画

Dolphin Books

海豚出版社　北京

First Edition 1989

一九八九年　第一版

ISBN 0-8351-2165-8 ISBN 7-80051-524-9 (P)
ISBN 0-8351-2169-0 ISBN 7-80051-523-0 (H)

Copyright 1989 by Dolphin Books, Beijing, China

Published by Dolphin Books,
24 Baiwanzhuang Road, Beijing, China

Distributed by China International Book Trading Corporation
(Guoji Shudian), P.O. Box 399, Beijing, China

Printed in the People's Republic of China

在中华人民共和国印刷

The mother sun was named Xi He. It is said that she gave birth to ten sons.

传说羲和生了十个小太阳。

They lived in a pond in the very far east, across the East Sea. In the middle of the pond there grew a large mulberry tree thousands of feet tall. What a beautiful scene.

他们住在东方的一个水池里。在水池的中央长着一棵高万丈、粗千尺的大桑树。

A big jade rooster dwelled on top of the tree.

桑树顶上站着一只玉鸡。

The ten brothers bathed and played in the pond, so the water was burning hot all the year round.

由于十个太阳兄弟每天都在水池里洗澡和玩耍，使得池水终年都是滚烫滚烫的。

At night, the ten young suns each slept on a branch of the tree.

夜里，十个太阳兄弟睡在桑树的十个枝杈上。

Tens of thousands of years passed before one day the mother asked her children to send their light and heat over the earth. They were all very joyful at this idea.

　　几万年过去了，羲和要十个儿子将光和热送到大地上去。儿子们听了十分高兴。

Early the next morning, when the jade rooster uttered its first crow, the mother and her first son set off in a dragon-pulled carriage.

第二天黎明，当玉鸡啼叫时，羲和和大儿子乘坐着龙车出发了。

The dragon wagon traveled from east to west for 153,730 miles, and light and heat covered the earth.

龙车在空中从东到西飞奔了五十万七千三百零九里，把光和热送给了大地。

The third morning, the mother traveled with her second son in the wagon from east to west along the route of the previous day...in this way the ten suns went on duty one by one, accompanied by their mother.

第三天一早，羲和又和二儿子坐着龙车，沿着昨天的路线从东向西奔去⋯⋯羲和就是这样每天不停地护送着十个儿子在天空奔跑着。

Thanks to the light and heat from the suns, the trees and crops grew stronger and the flowers put on a brighter color. Everything was full of life.

大地由于有了太阳的光和热，树木庄稼更绿了，花儿也更红了，到处生机勃勃。

People expressed their sincere gratitude to the suns.

人们衷心感谢太阳送来的光明和温暖。

One night, the ten brothers gathered and talked with keen pleasure about what they had seen during the day. "Let's go together tomorrow morning," suggested the youngest, still a naughty boy. Everyone agreed to it.

一天晚上，太阳兄弟在一起津津有味地谈论着白天看到的许多美景，顽皮的小弟弟说："明天我们一齐出去，好吗？"大家同意了。

At daybreak, the ten brothers got ready and all started to run from east to west. No matter how their mother called they never turned back.

第二天清晨，十个太阳兄弟一齐出发，由东向西奔跑。羲和大声制止，他们也不回头。

They danced and cried with joy, blowing out flames from their mouths.

他们在空中喷吐着火焰，跳呀，蹦呀，可乐呢!

As a result calamity befell the earth. Plants were burnt, rivers dried up, and people had a difficult time. High temperatures made the air hard to breathe. People had nowhere else to go, so they sheltered themselves in caves.

　　这么一来，大地可遭殃了，庄稼晒死了，花儿晒枯了，河水也干了，人们热得喘不过气，躲进了山洞。

Chief Rao Huang called his people to their knees to plead for the suns' departure, but the ten brothers refused to listen. Instead, they merrily spurted even more flames.

首领尧皇带着人们跪求太阳离开，可是太阳兄弟谁也不听，反而将火焰越吐越旺。

Rao Huang cried desperately at the sight of his people struggling in thirst and hunger.

尧皇看到不少人在饥渴中垂死挣扎，不禁失声痛哭起来。

The image of Hou Yi the archer suddenly flashed in his mind. Without delay he sent for him, deep in the mountains.

这时，尧皇想起了射箭能手后羿，连忙派人到深山去将他请来。

Hou Yi was a master archer. He could hit a target as small as a leaf from 30 miles away.

后羿的箭法可好啦，能在百里以外射中他要射的一片树叶。

He said goodbye to his dear wife and set off immediately.

后羿告别了心爱的妻子嫦娥出发了。

On the way he was filled with great sorrow at the sight of the many dead bodies on the ground and indignation at the cheering and playing of the suns in the sky.

一路上他看到许多尸体，又听见天上的十个太阳在嬉闹，心里悲愤交加。

Hou Yi scolded them for the disaster they had caused by coming out all at once and demanded that they return home right away. No response. He exploded with anger.

后羿指责十个太阳不该一齐跑出来，烧伤了万物，请他们赶快回去。可是，十个太阳没一个理睬他。后羿气极了。

Without another word, Hou Yi took out an arrow, bent the bow, aimed at the eldest sun and released the bowstring.

说时迟，那时快，只听到"嗖"的一声，后羿拉开弓对准太阳老大射去。

Zap! The white arrow hit its target. The eldest brother exploded in a ball of fire and fell from the sky, leaving a long trail of smoke.

"轰"的一声巨响，太阳老大被箭射中了。只见天上流火乱飞，太阳老大冒着一股浓烟摇摇晃晃地掉了下来。

While the other suns were stunned, the second and third brothers were shot down, giving out their last cries.

正当其他九个太阳惊呆的时候，后羿又连放两箭，太阳老二和老三又被他射下来了。

People looked up and saw the two falling fireballs change into two big three-clawed ravens.

当这两个太阳坠落时，人们看到两个大火球变成了两只长着三只脚的大乌鸦。

With a loud boom two black hills rose where the ravens dropped to the ground.

两只大乌鸦落到地上时发出一声巨响，随即变成了两座黑石山。

The remaining seven suns flied into such a rage that they fiercely shot fire all over the earth with all their might.

剩下的七个太阳象发了疯似的一齐向大地猛喷火焰。

Resisting the flaming waves of air, Hou Yi prepared for the fourth shot. Zap! Another was killed.

后羿顶着一股股热浪，继续拉弓射箭。"轰"的一声巨响，又一只太阳被他射中。

The ones left alive were scared and tried to run away.

这下可把其余的六个太阳吓慌啦，他们赶忙逃走。

Hou Yi followed close behind on horseback, killing five others one by one.

后羿骑着马紧紧追上去，又接二连三地射下了五个太阳。

Sputtering smoke, the five suns dropped into the sea and turned into rocks and islands.

冒着浓烟的五个太阳纷纷掉进大海里，变成了礁石和岛屿。

Suddenly a bolt shot out from the blue, followed by a storm of rain. The air became cool and fresh. People finally came out of their cave shelters, cheering and dancing in utmost joy.

　突然，晴天霹雳，下了一场大雨，气候凉爽了。人们纷纷从洞里跑出来，欢呼着。

By now, the last sun could not run any farther. He shrank back
and trembled with fear, his face pale.

这时，天上仅剩下的一个太阳早已吓白了脸，在那里发抖呢!

Hou Yi was about to finish the battle with one last shot when Rao Huang stopped him.

当后羿正拉弓要射第十个太阳的时候，被尧皇喊住。

"People need light and warmth for life, so leave him for the sake
of the human world."

尧皇对他说:"人们生活需要光明和温暖，留下他普照人间吧!"

It became as cool and fresh and humid as before. The earth came back to life. Crops turned green and flowers bloomed.

　　气候已变得和先前一样凉爽、湿润。庄稼复活了，花儿吐艳了，大地上万物苏醒了。

Ever since then, Hou Yi's brave deeds had been praised and his name passed on generation after generation.

人们夸奖后羿，他射日除害的事迹一直传颂到今天。